CALLIGRAPHY PAPER

120 Pages

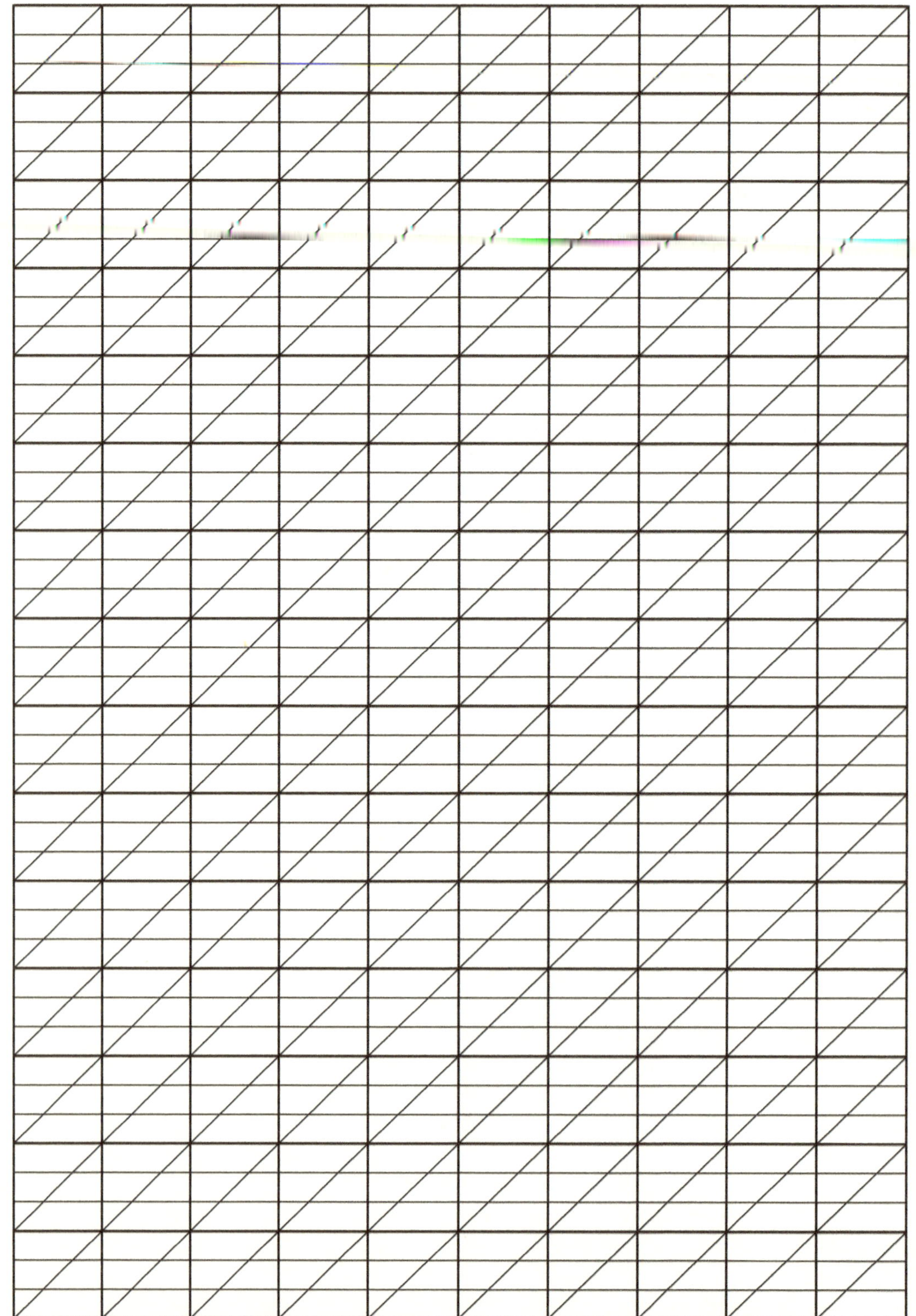

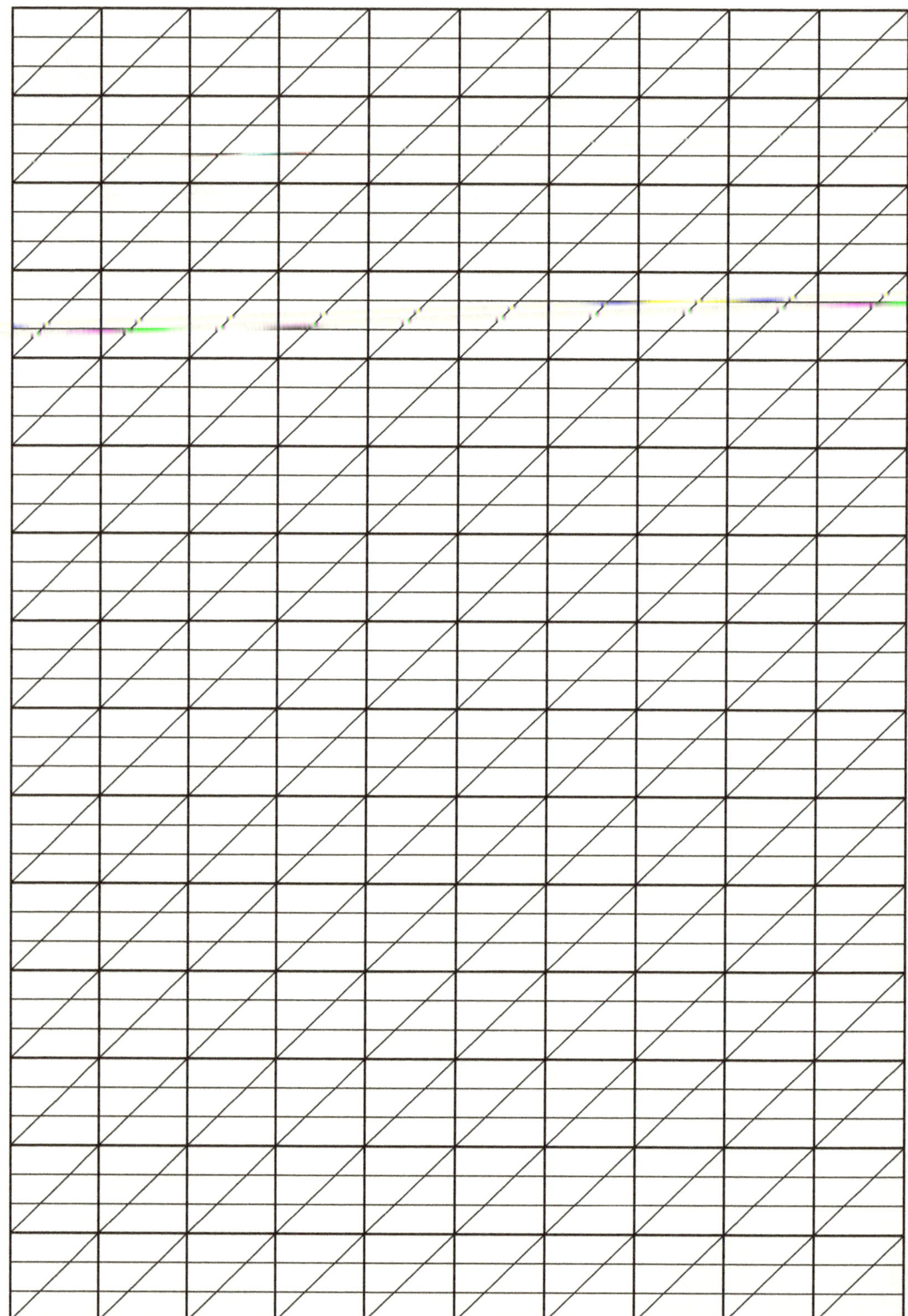

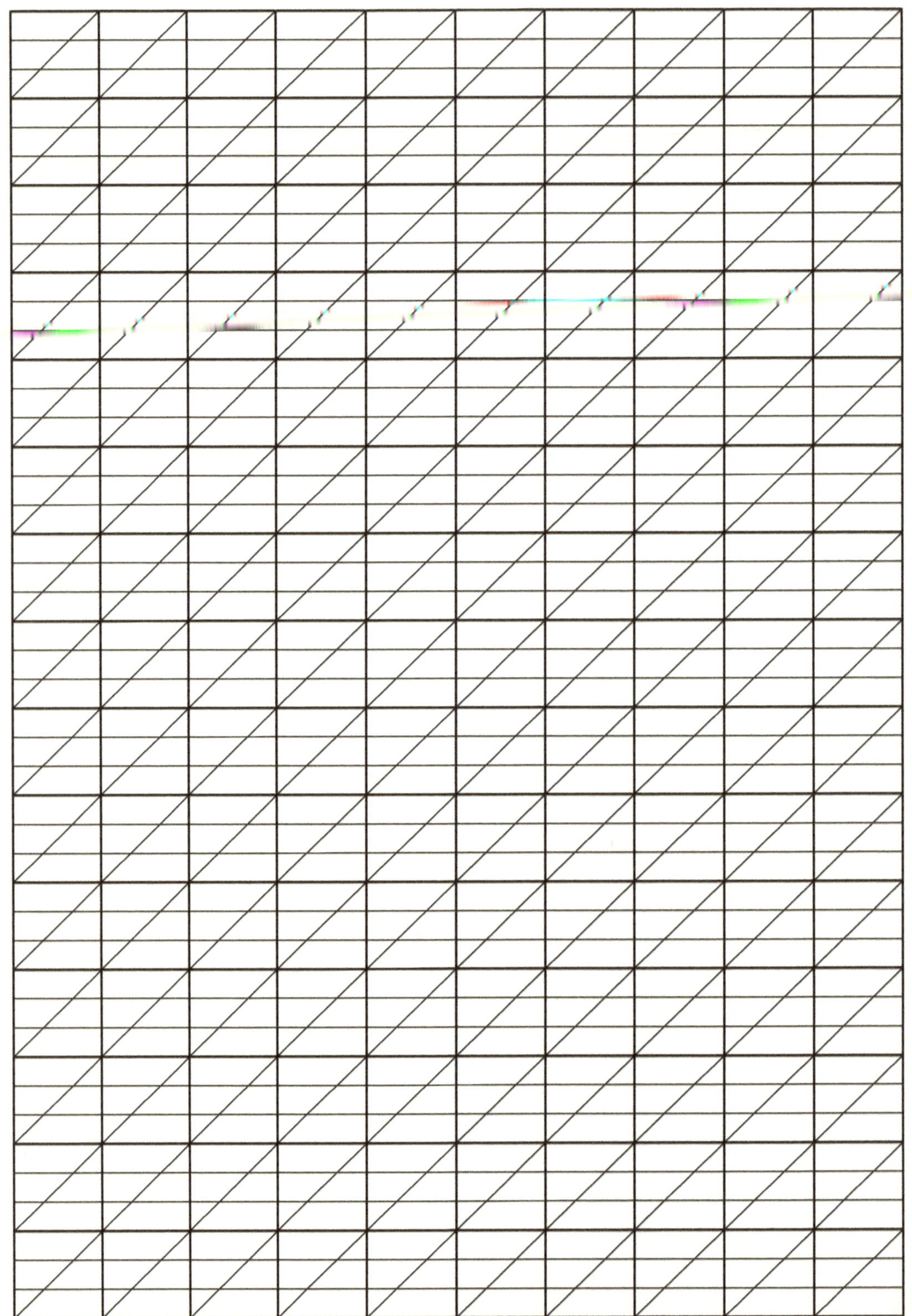

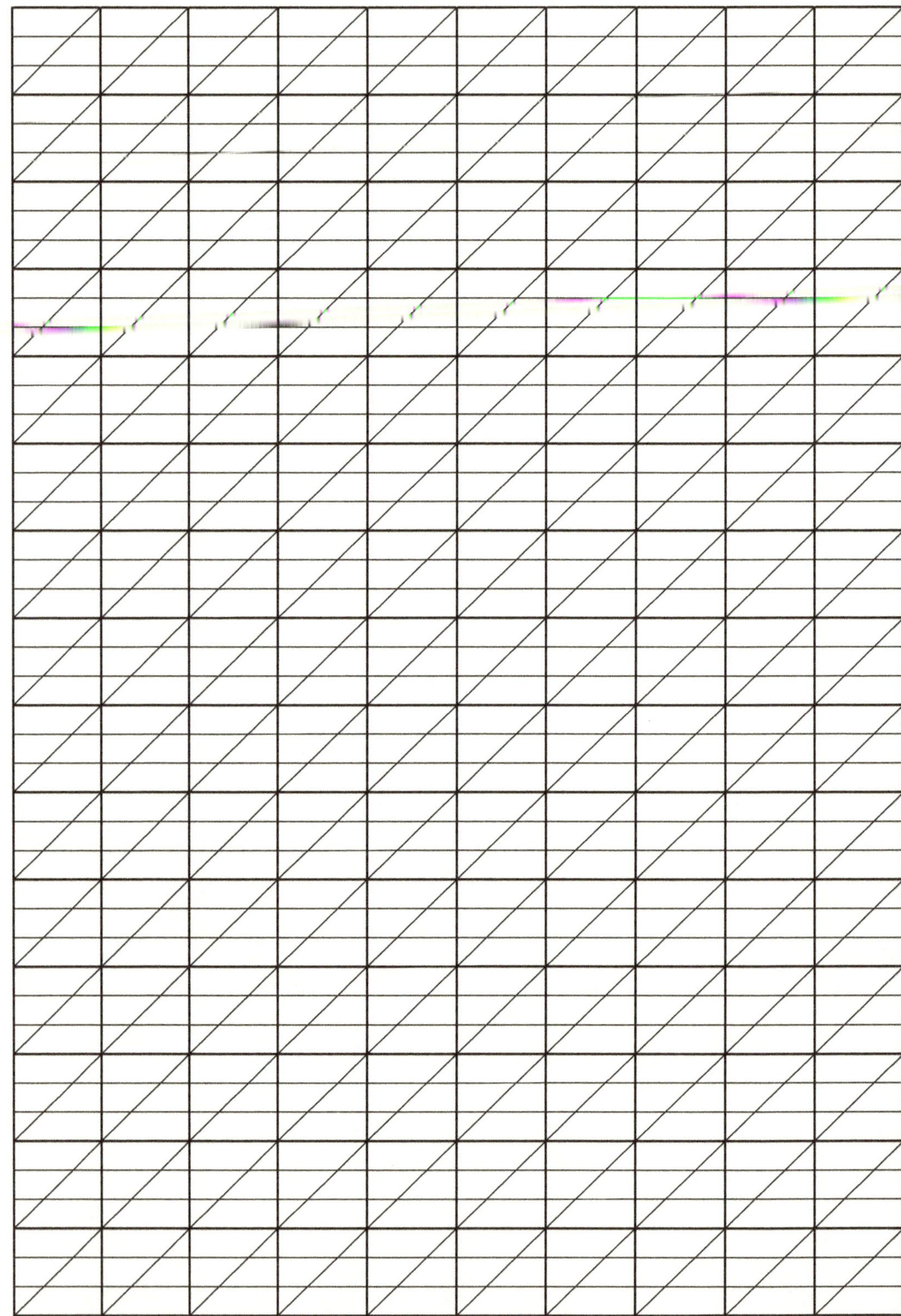

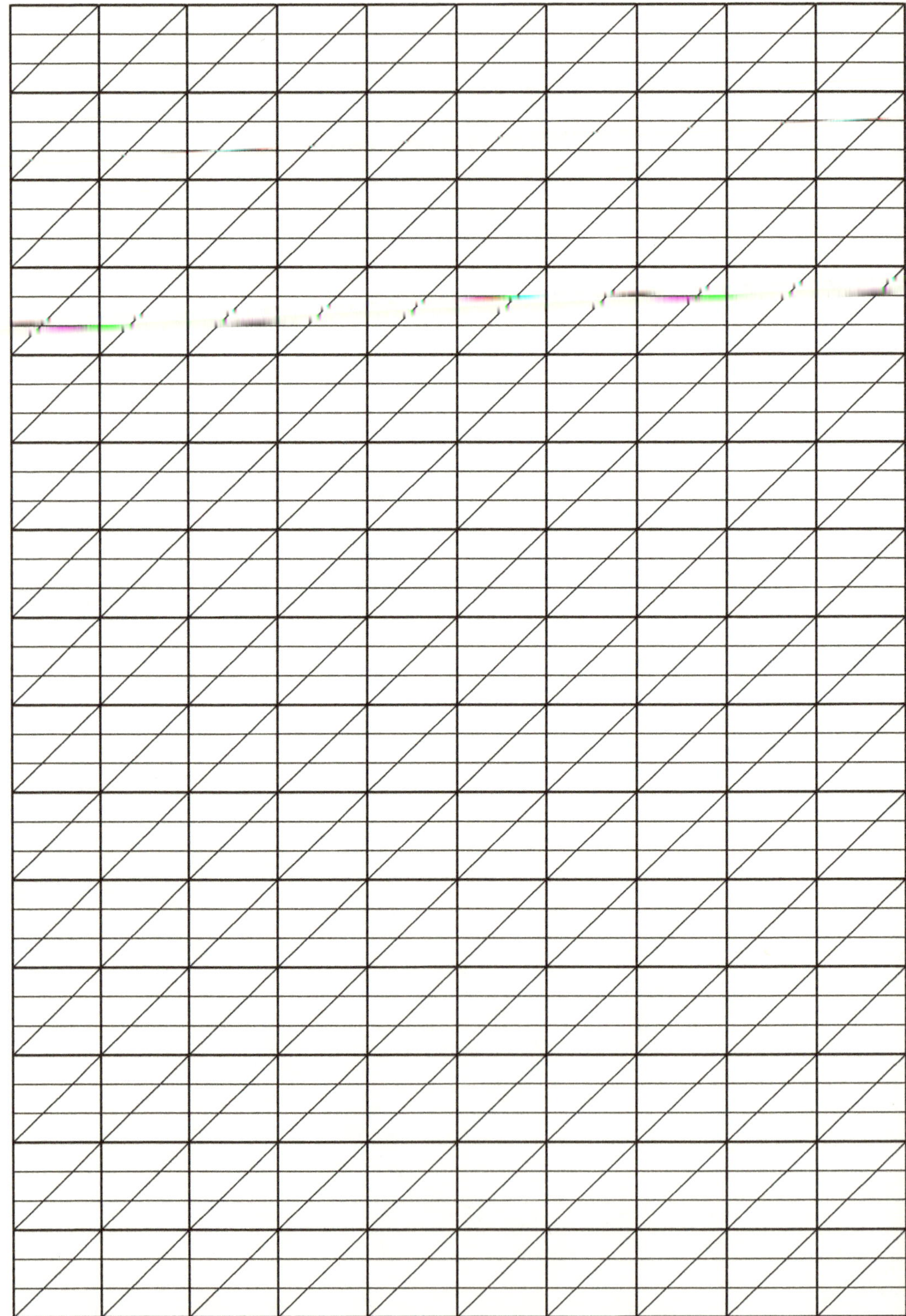

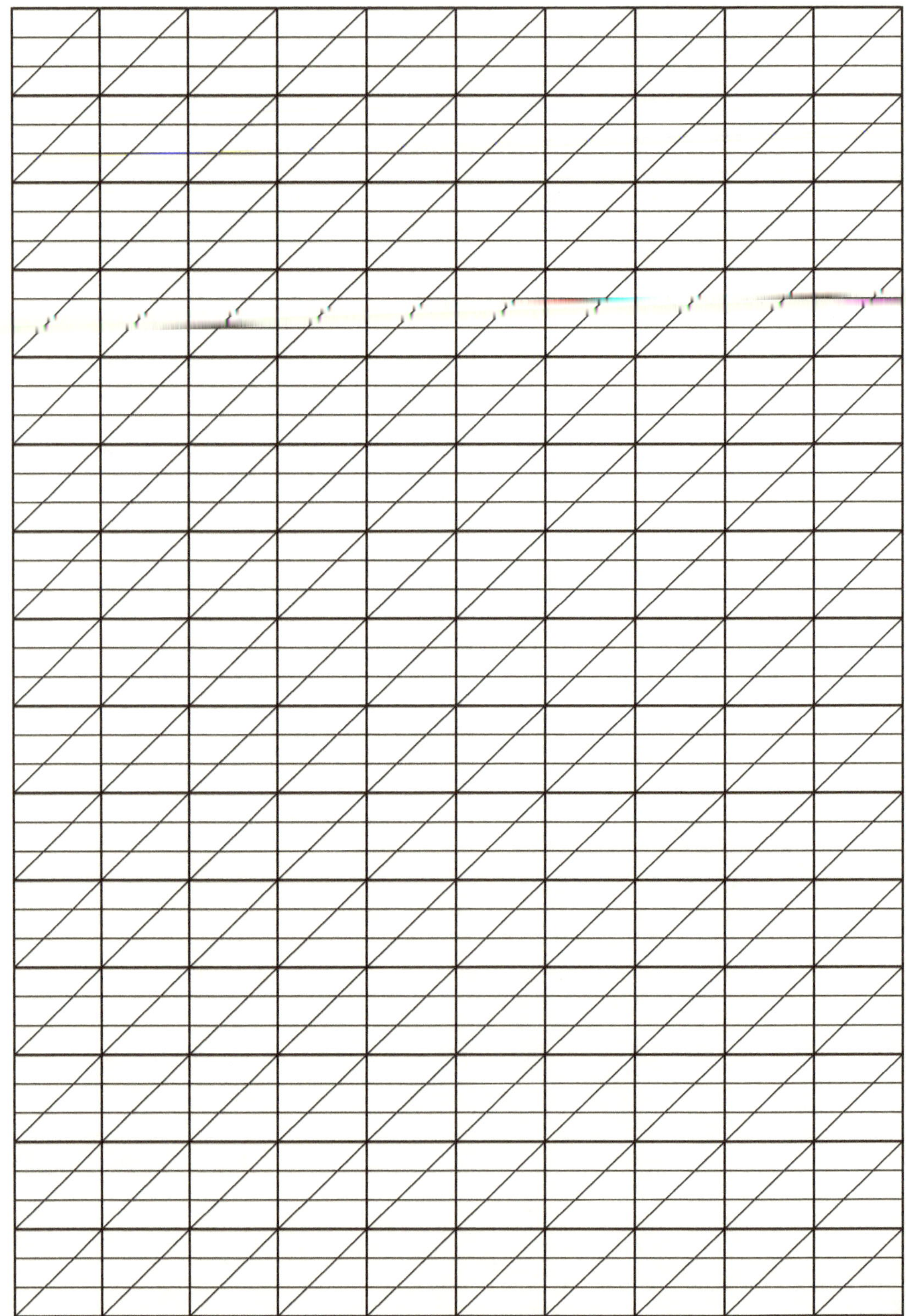

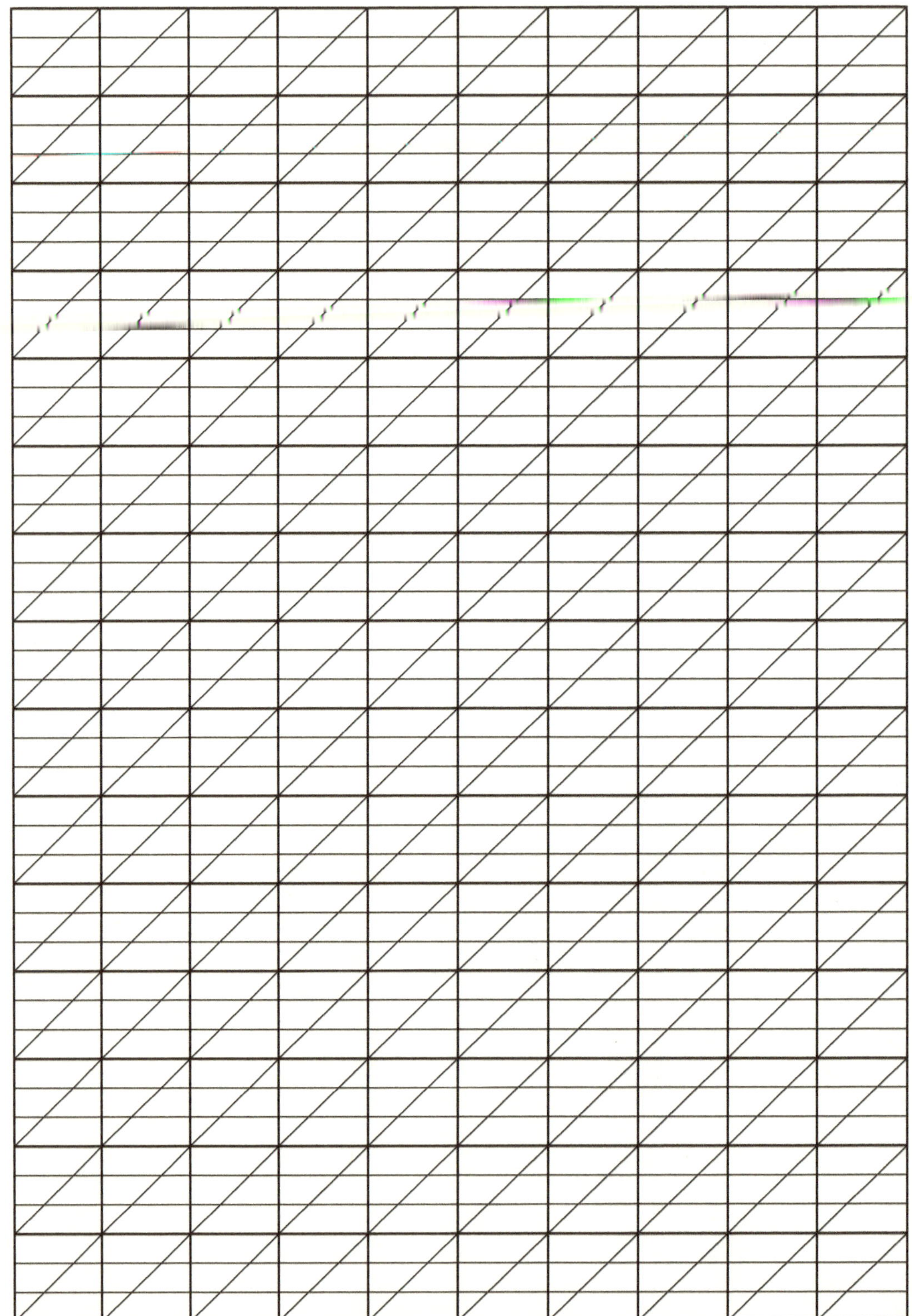

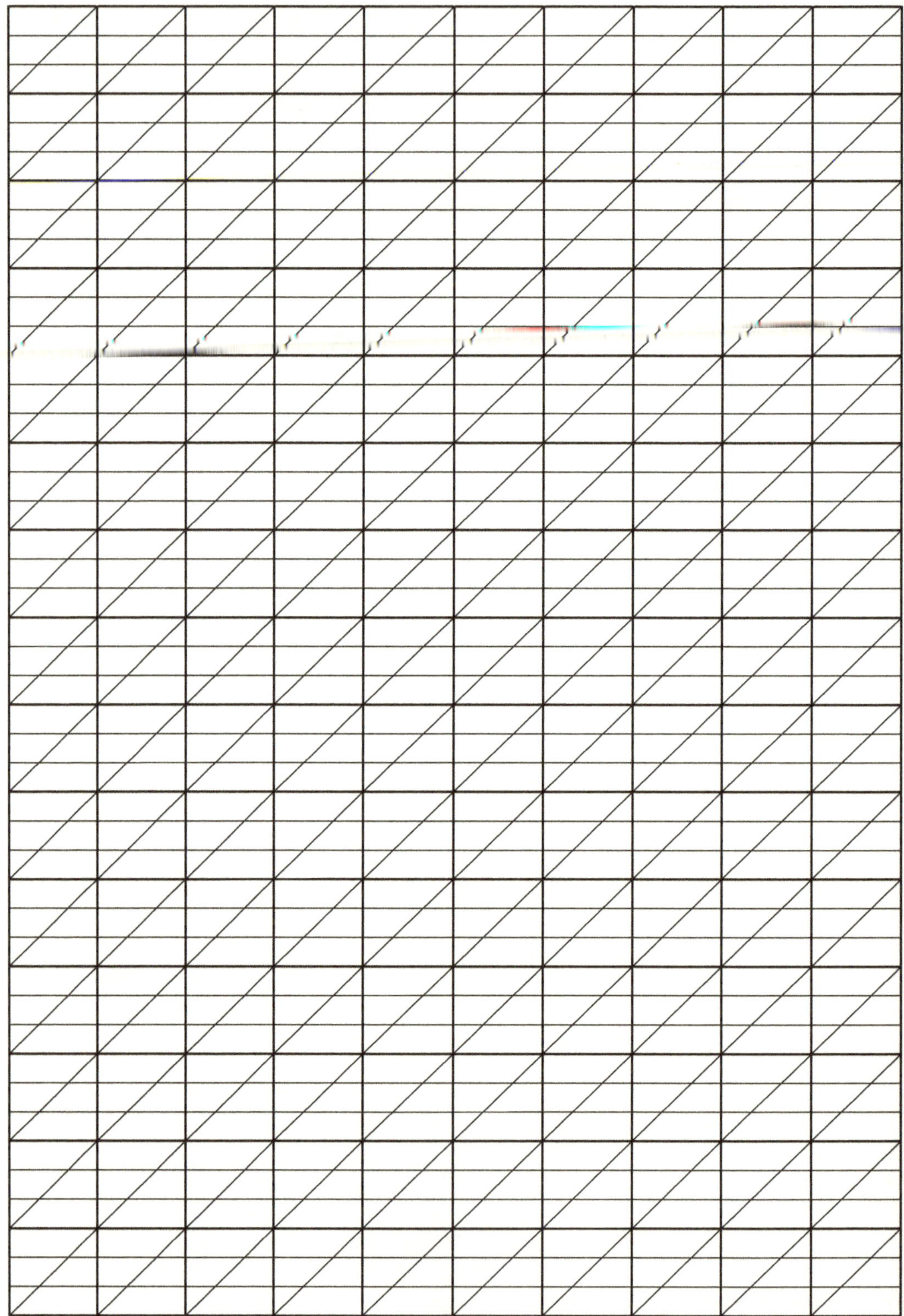

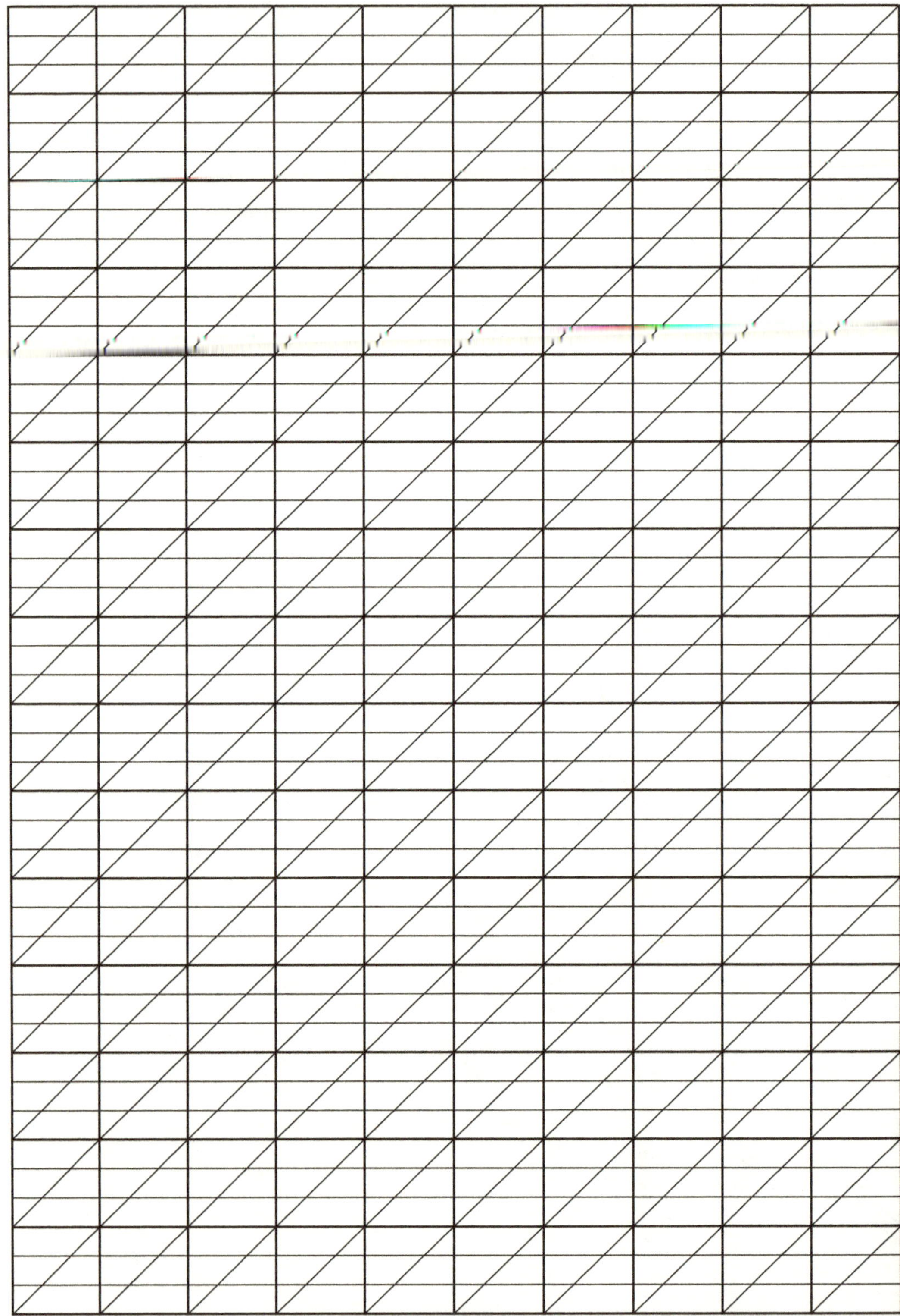

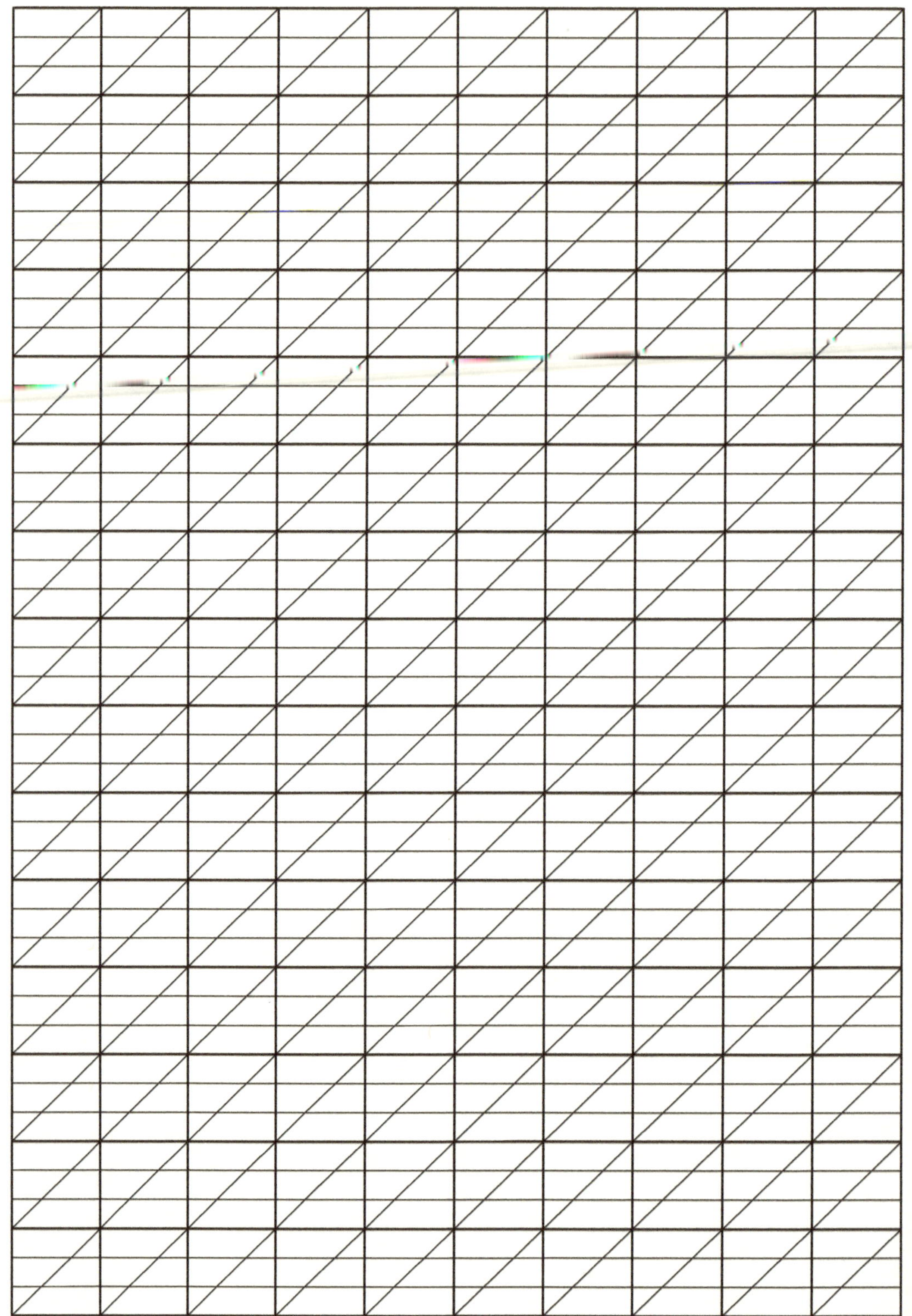

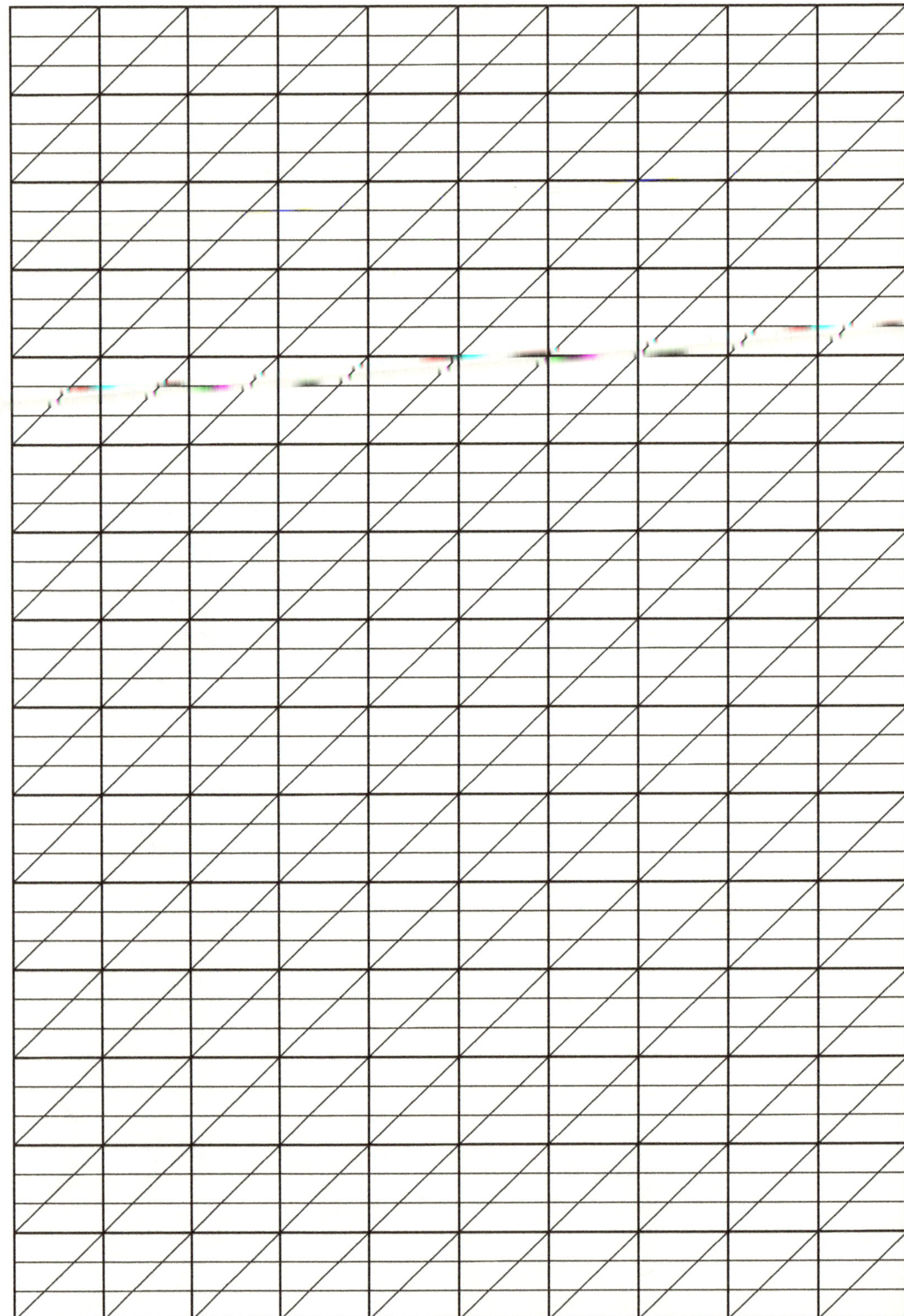

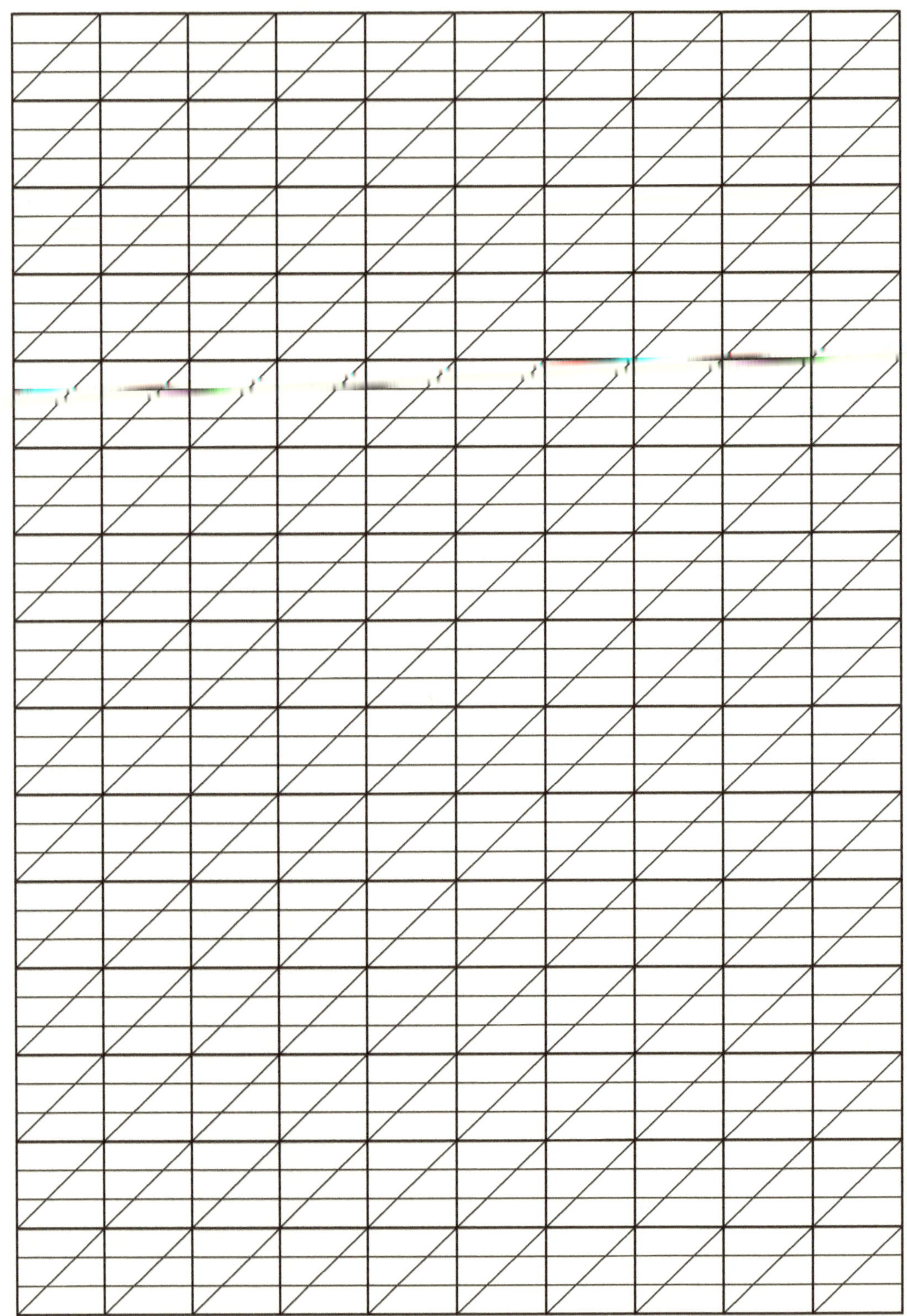

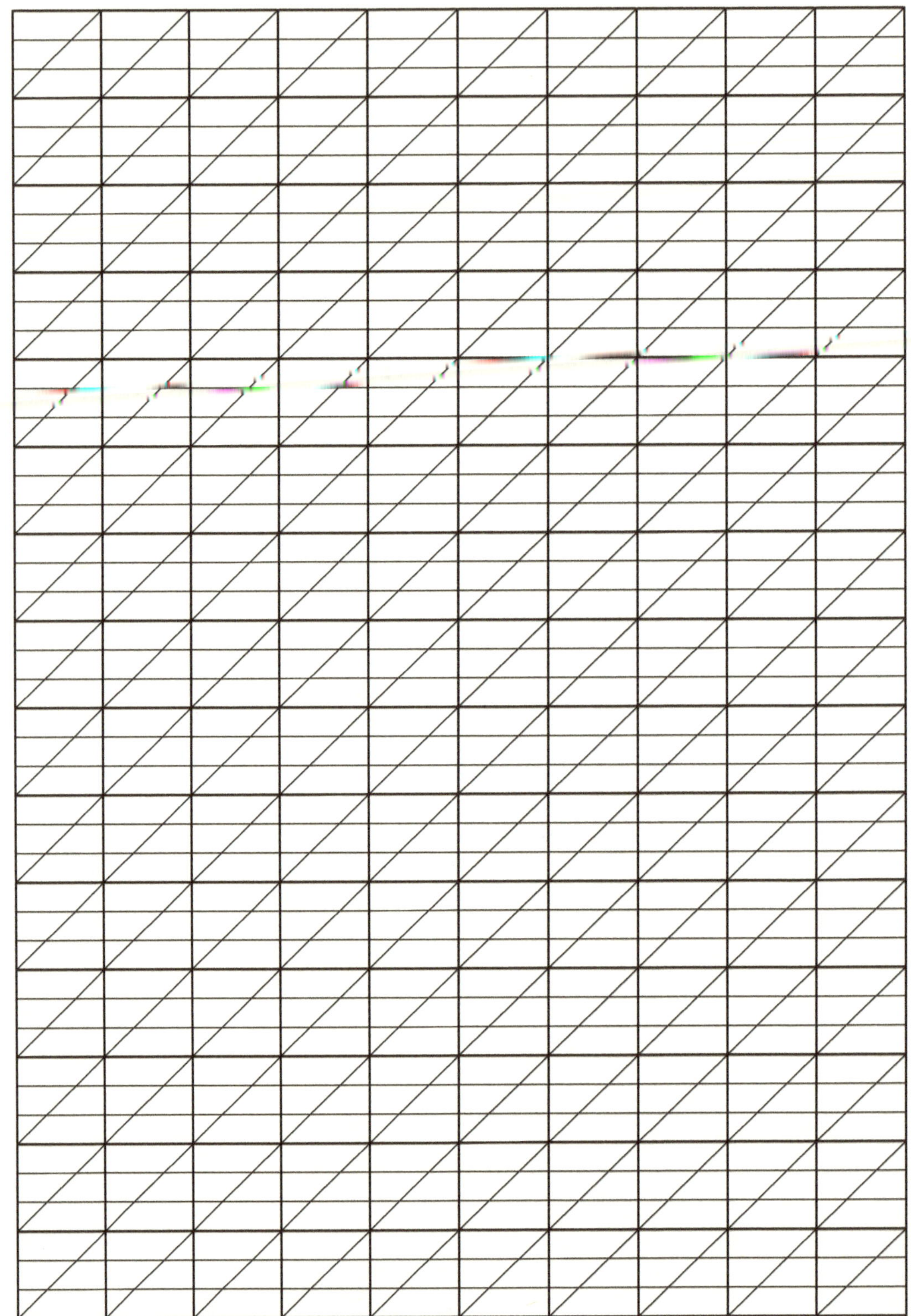

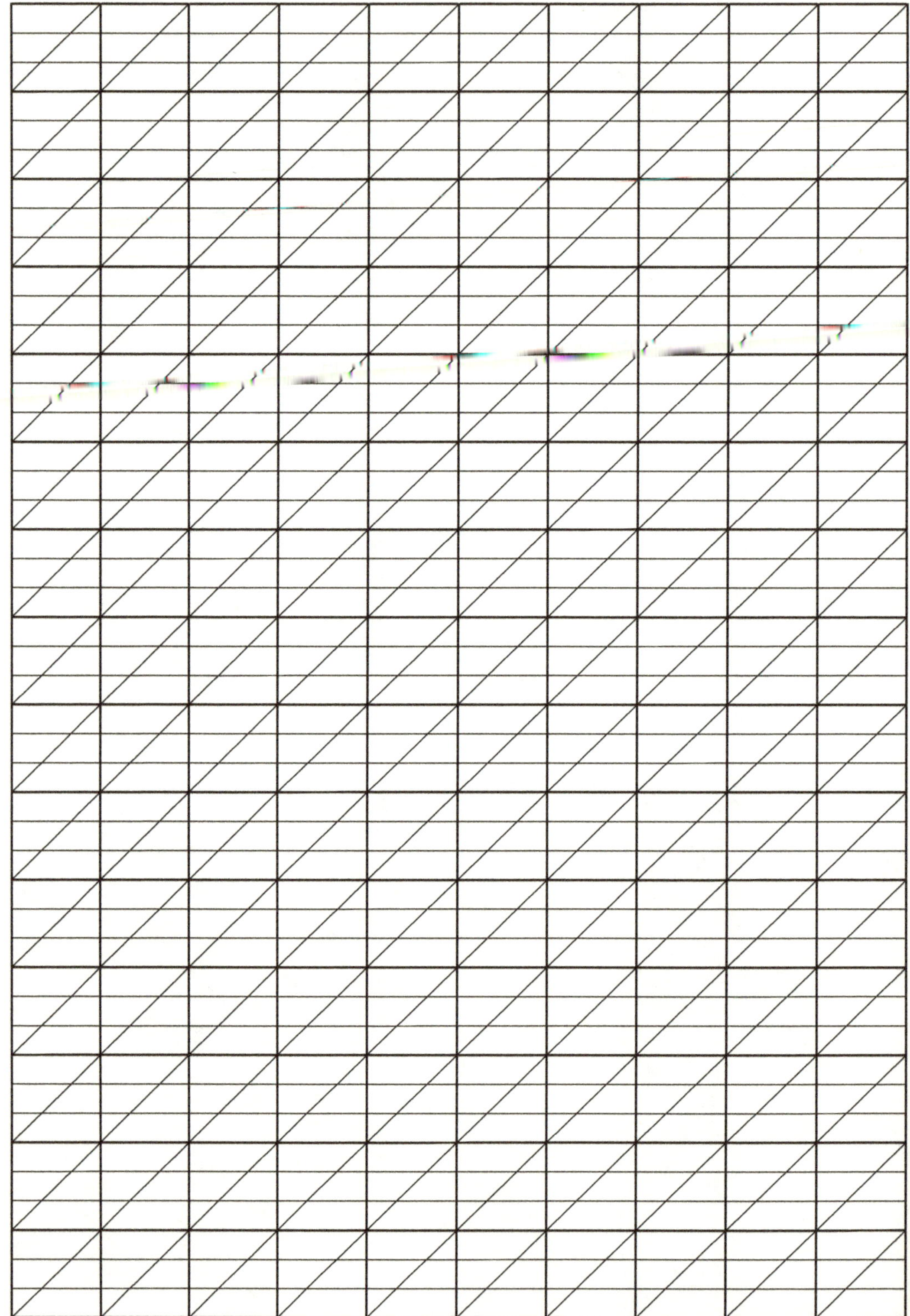

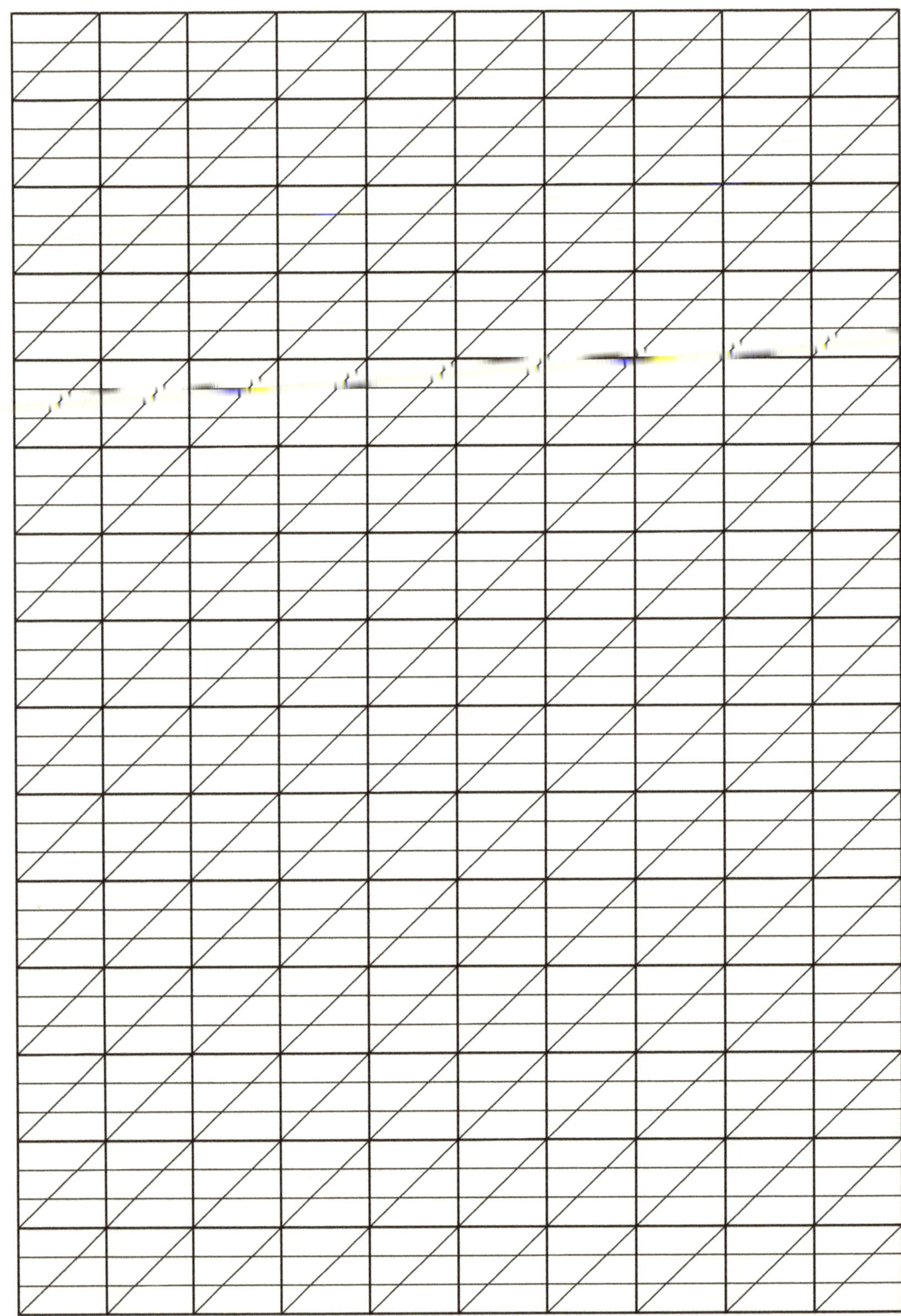

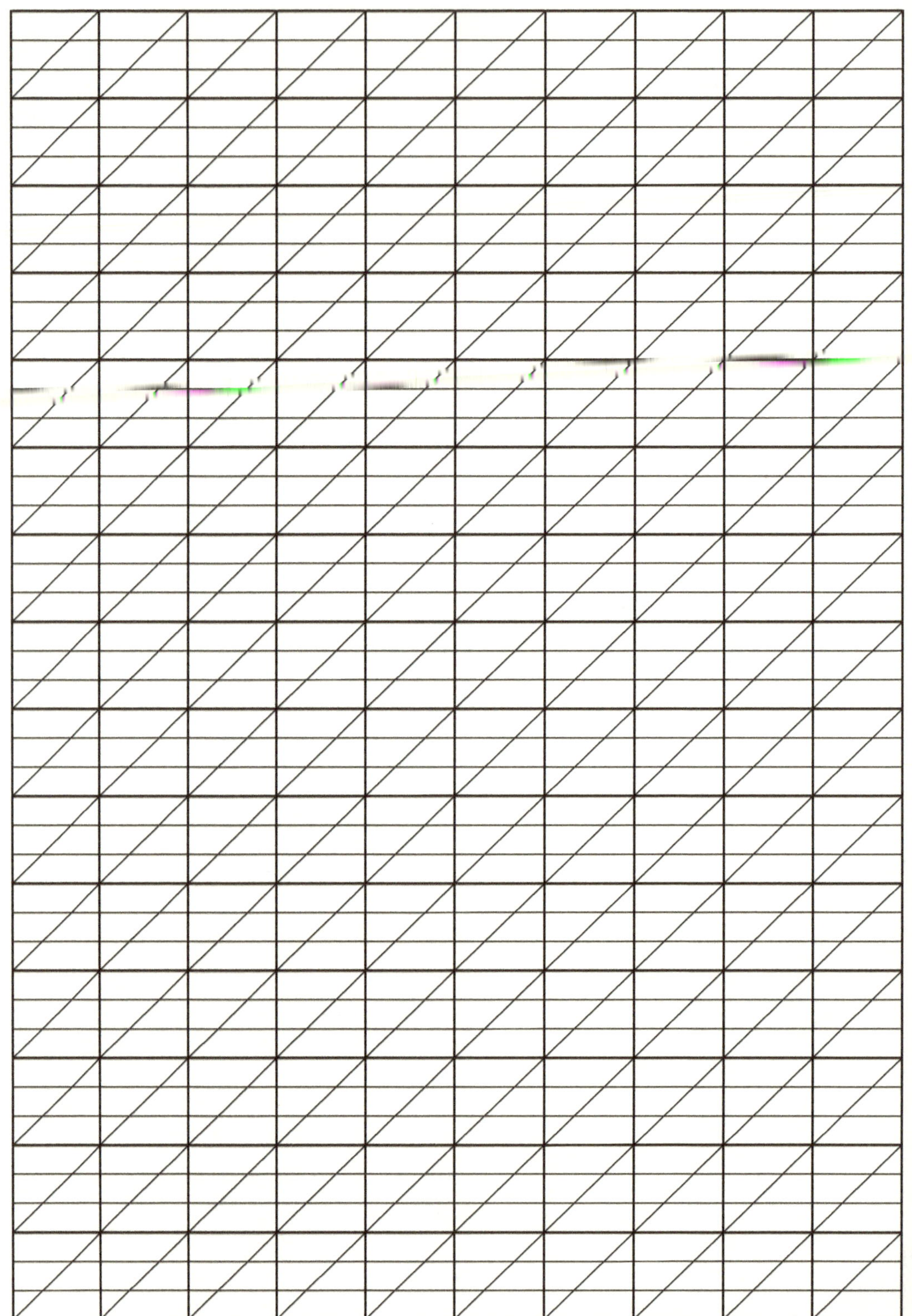

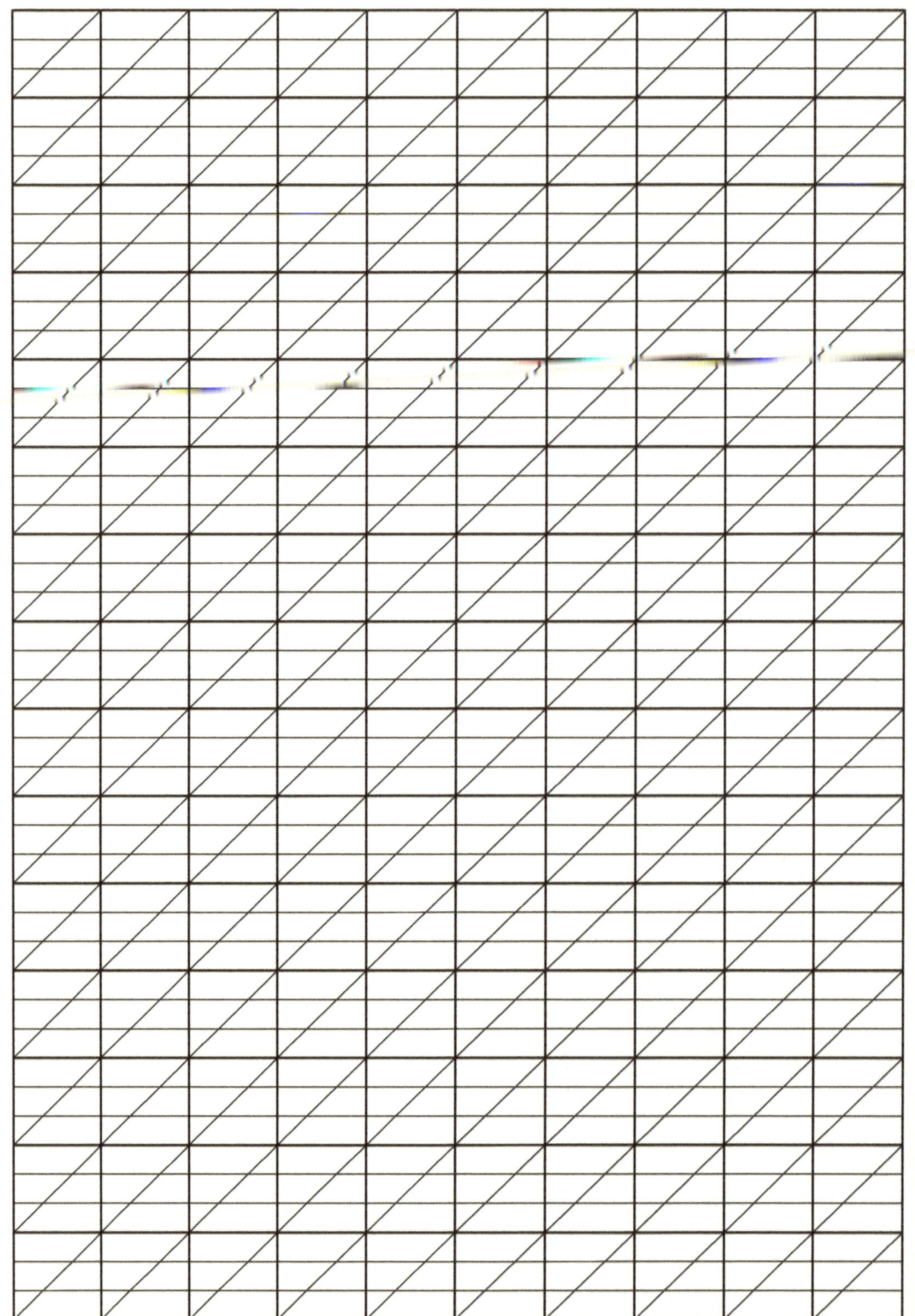

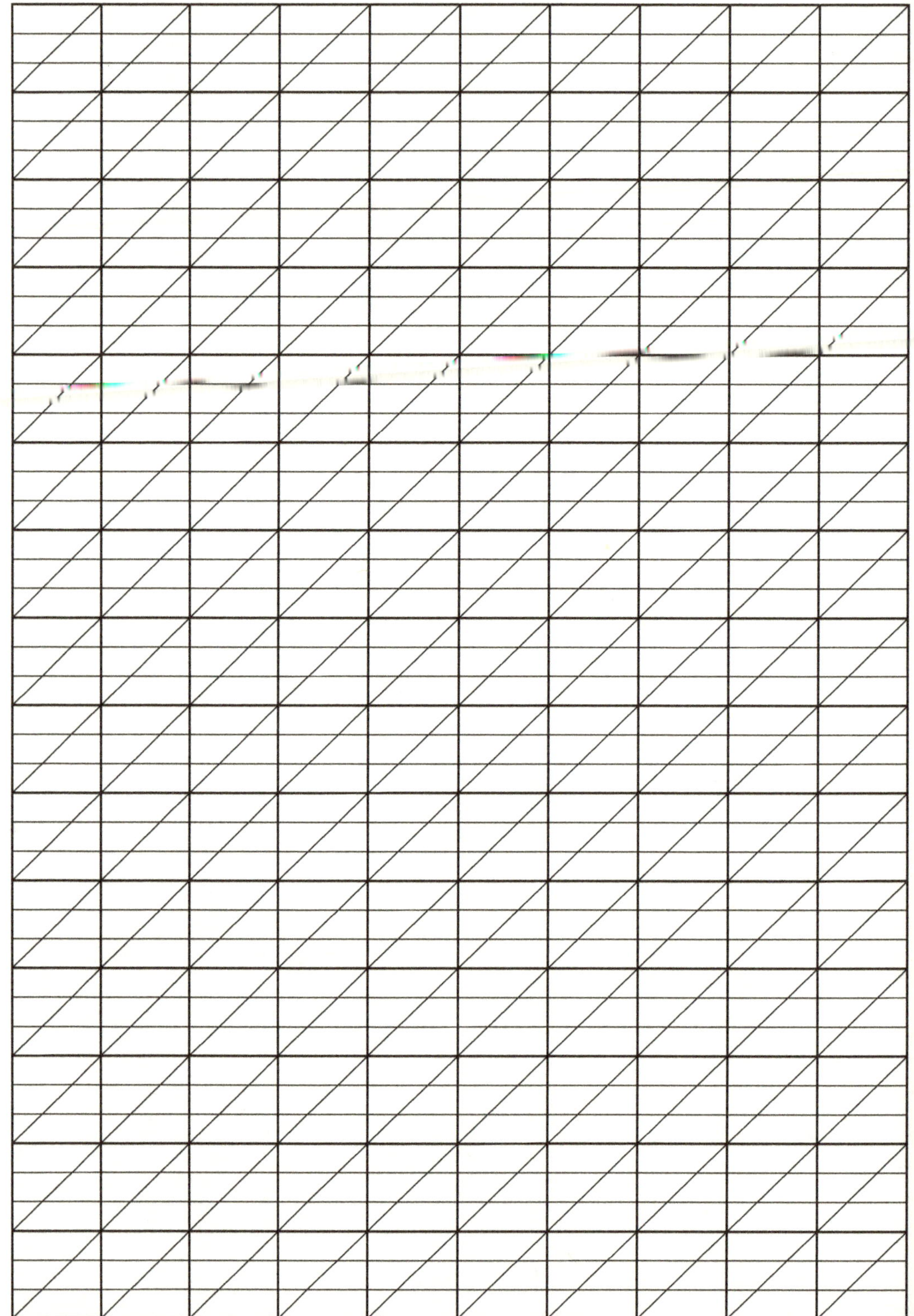

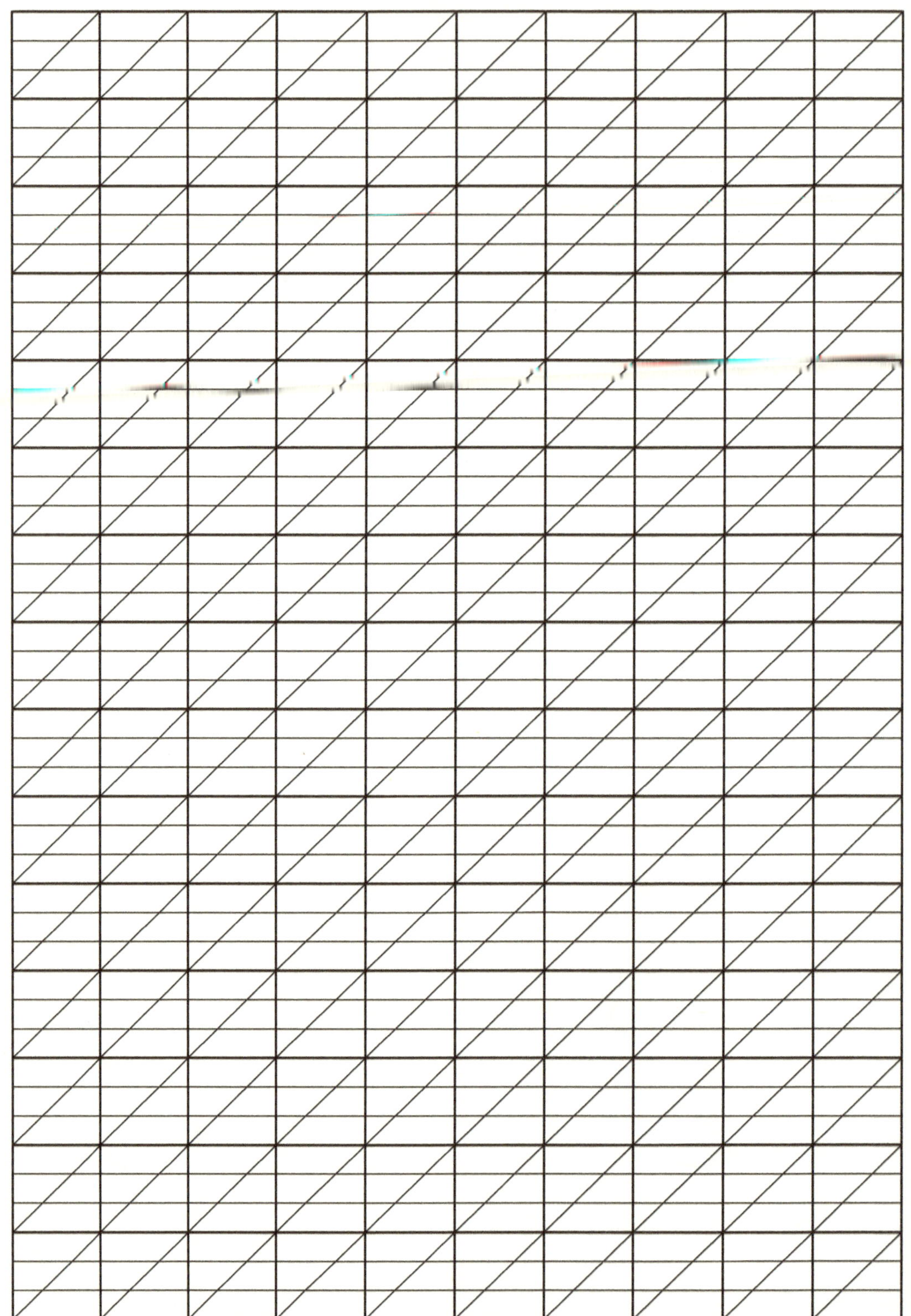

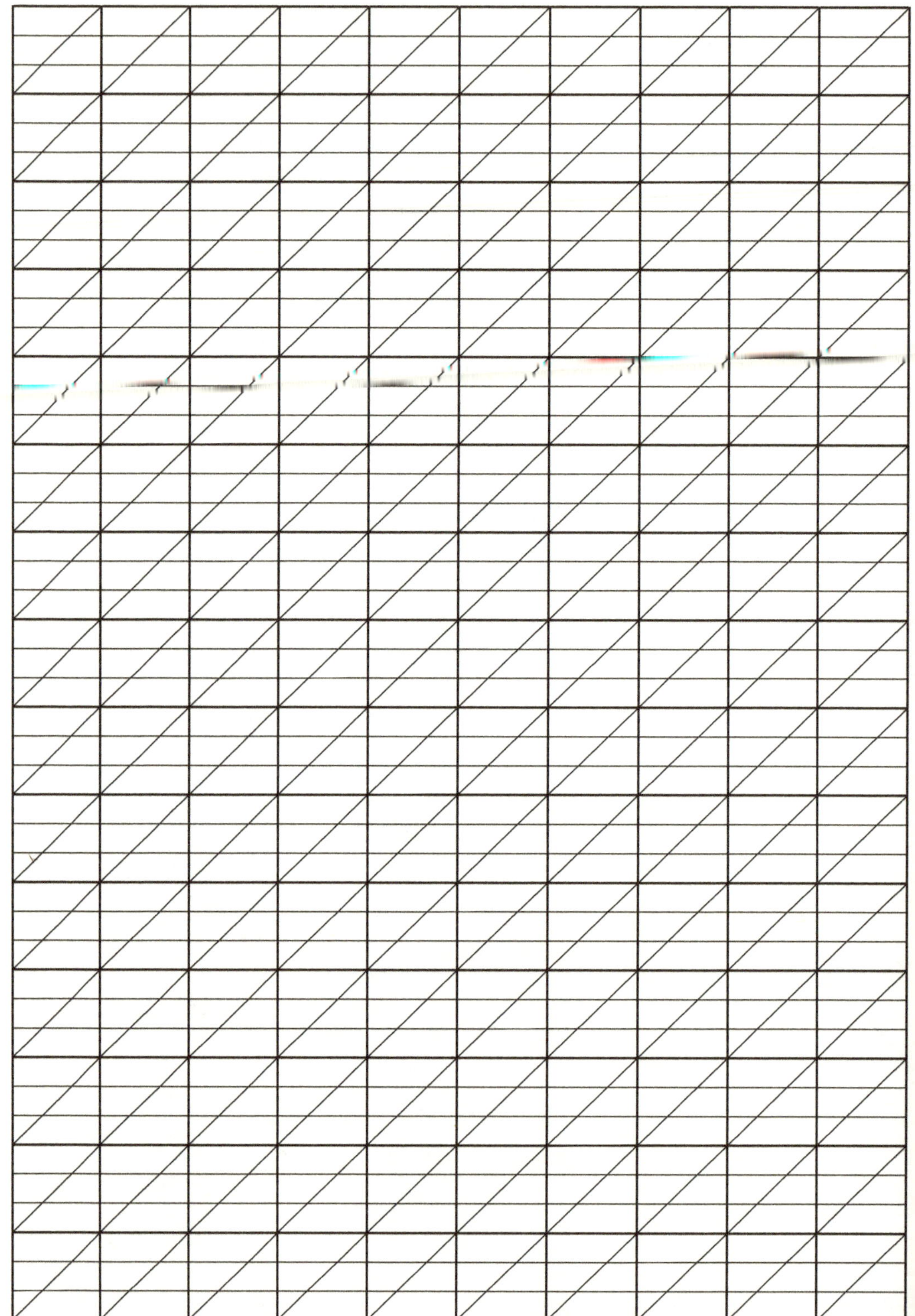

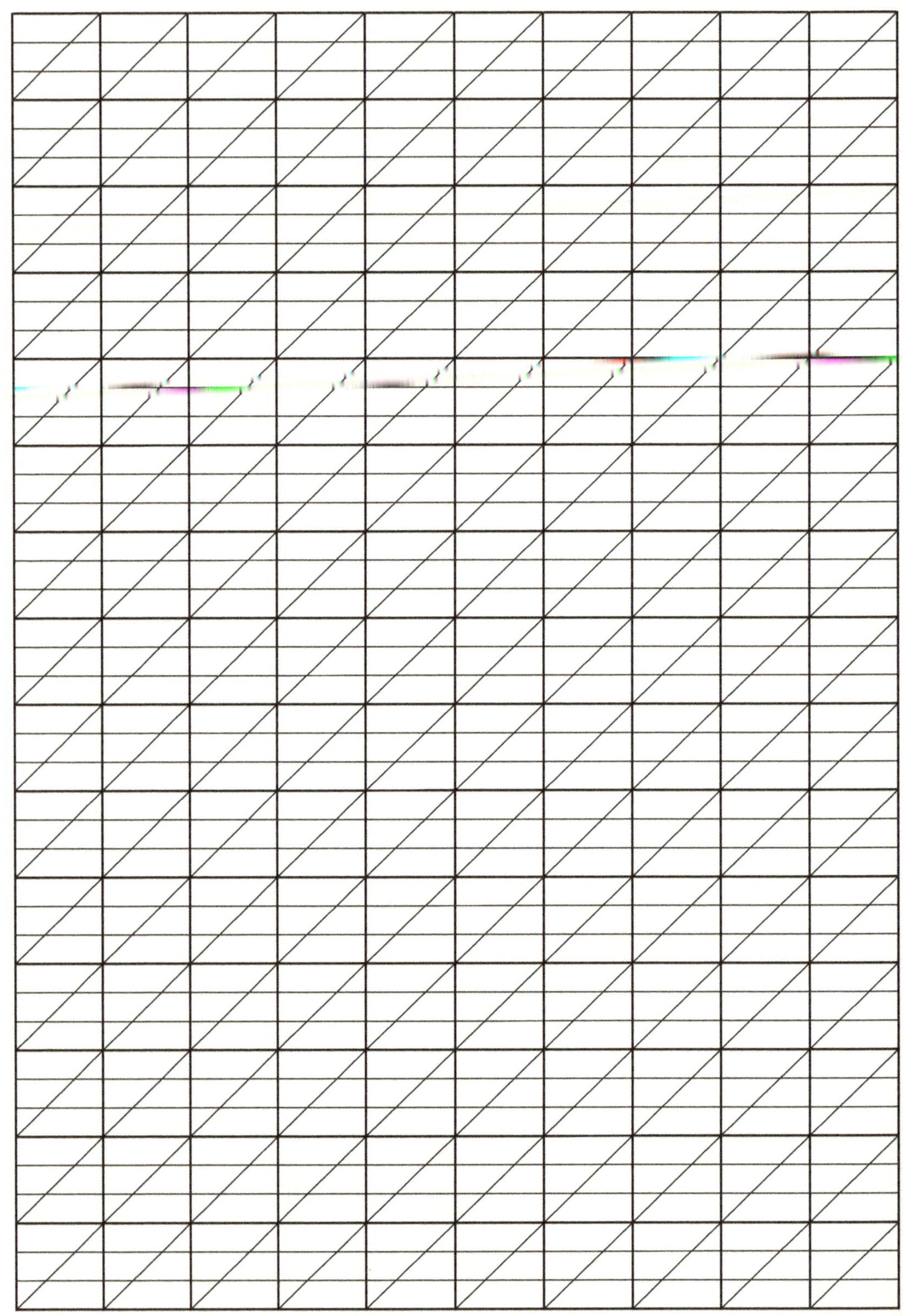

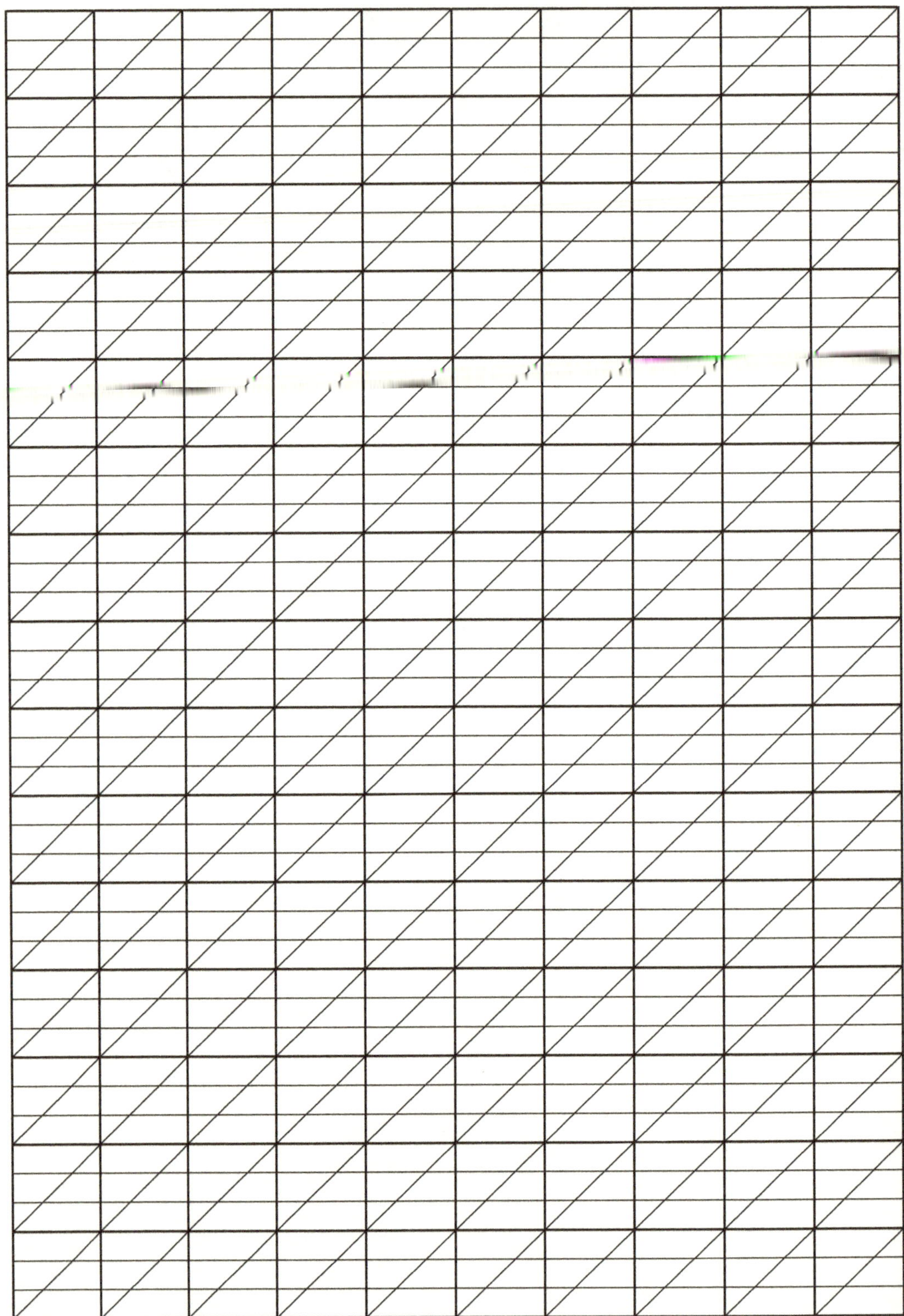

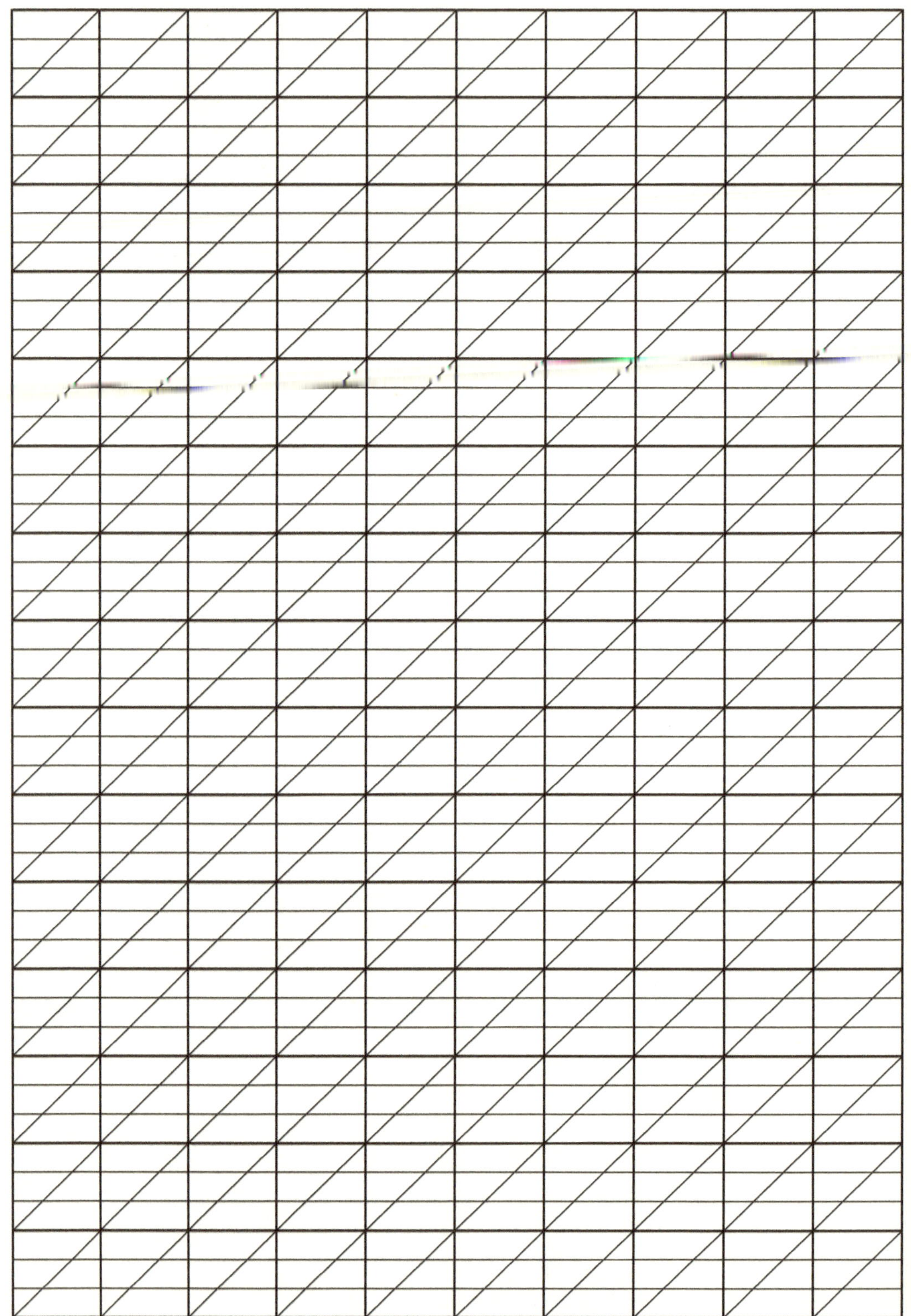

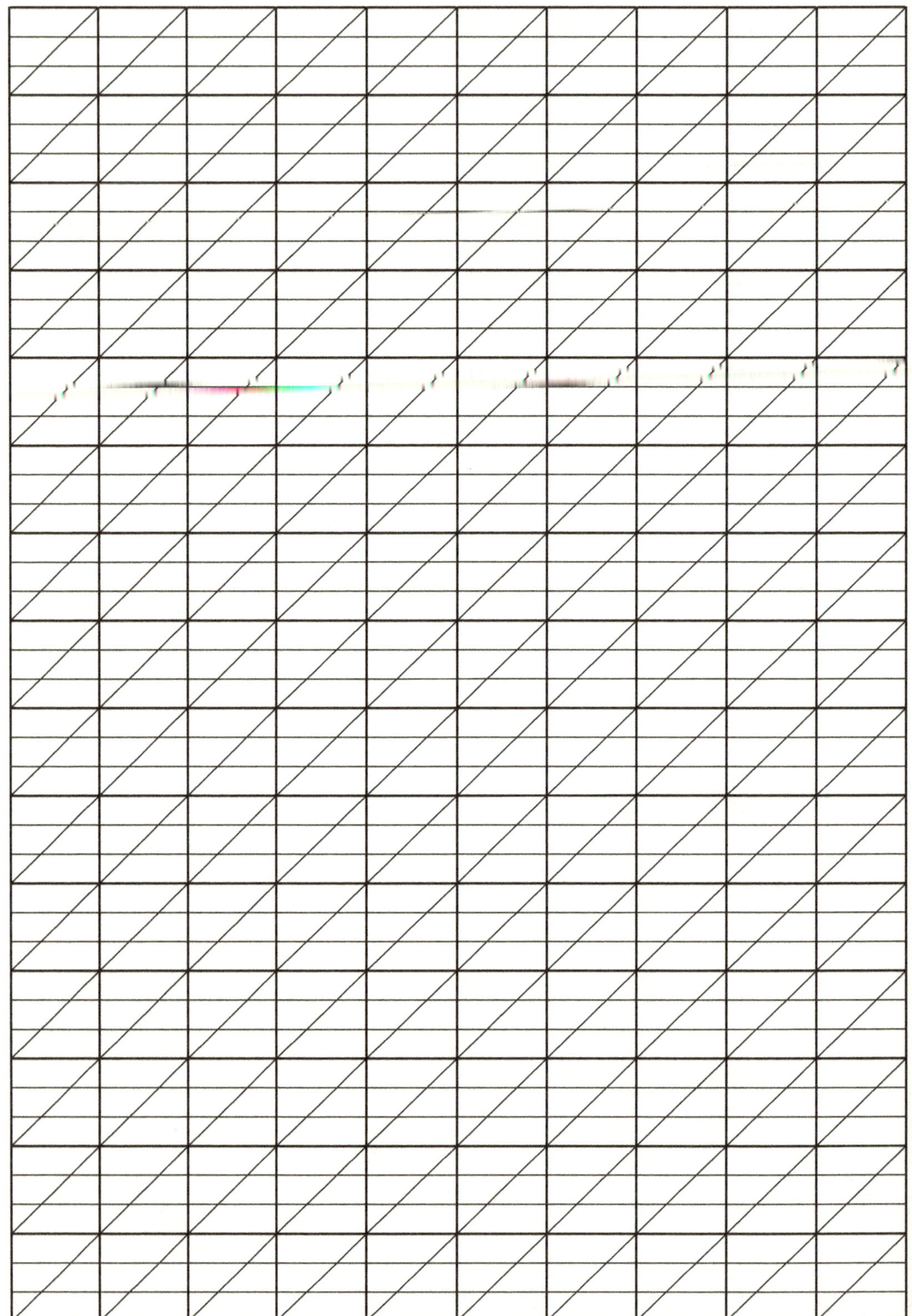

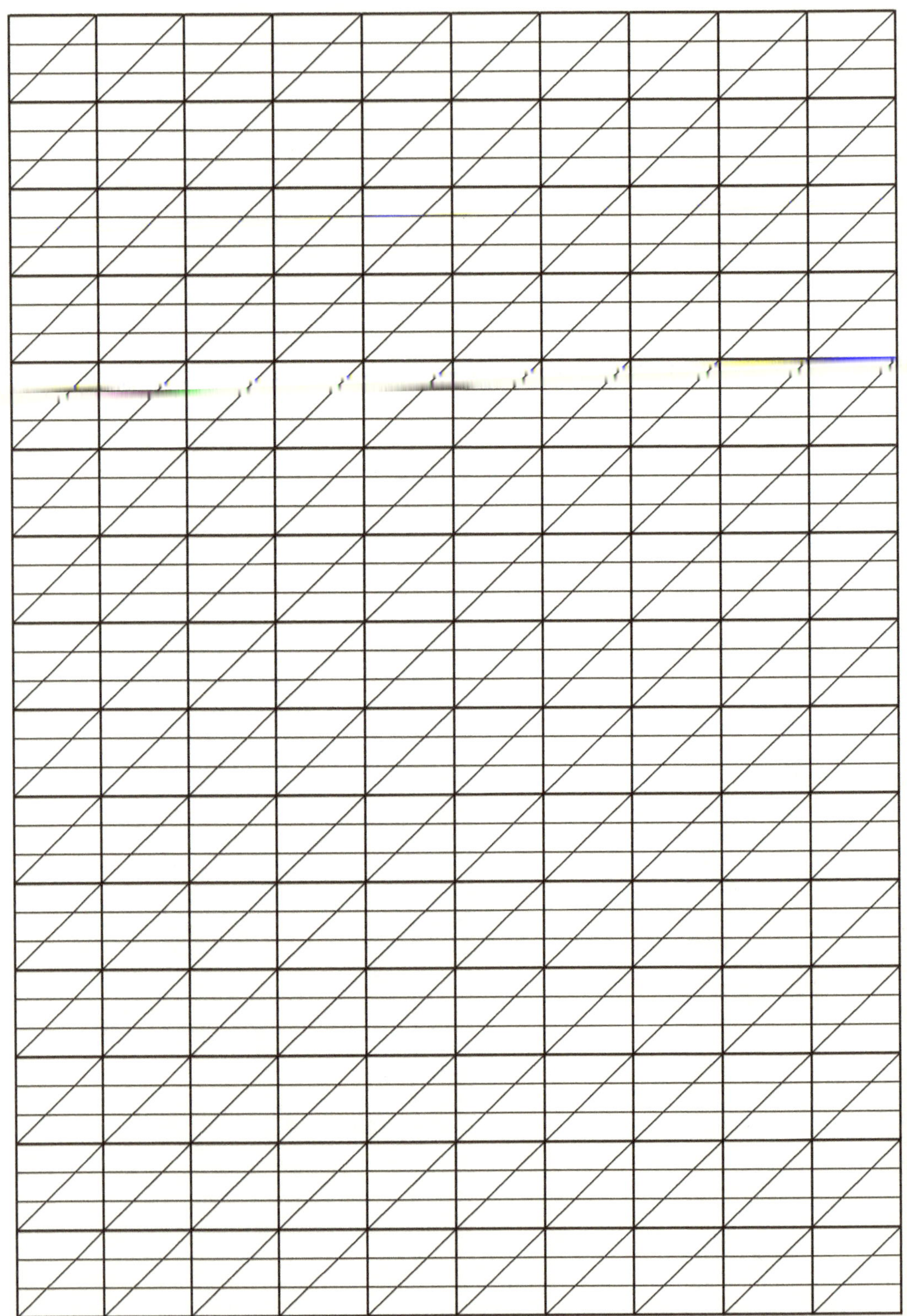

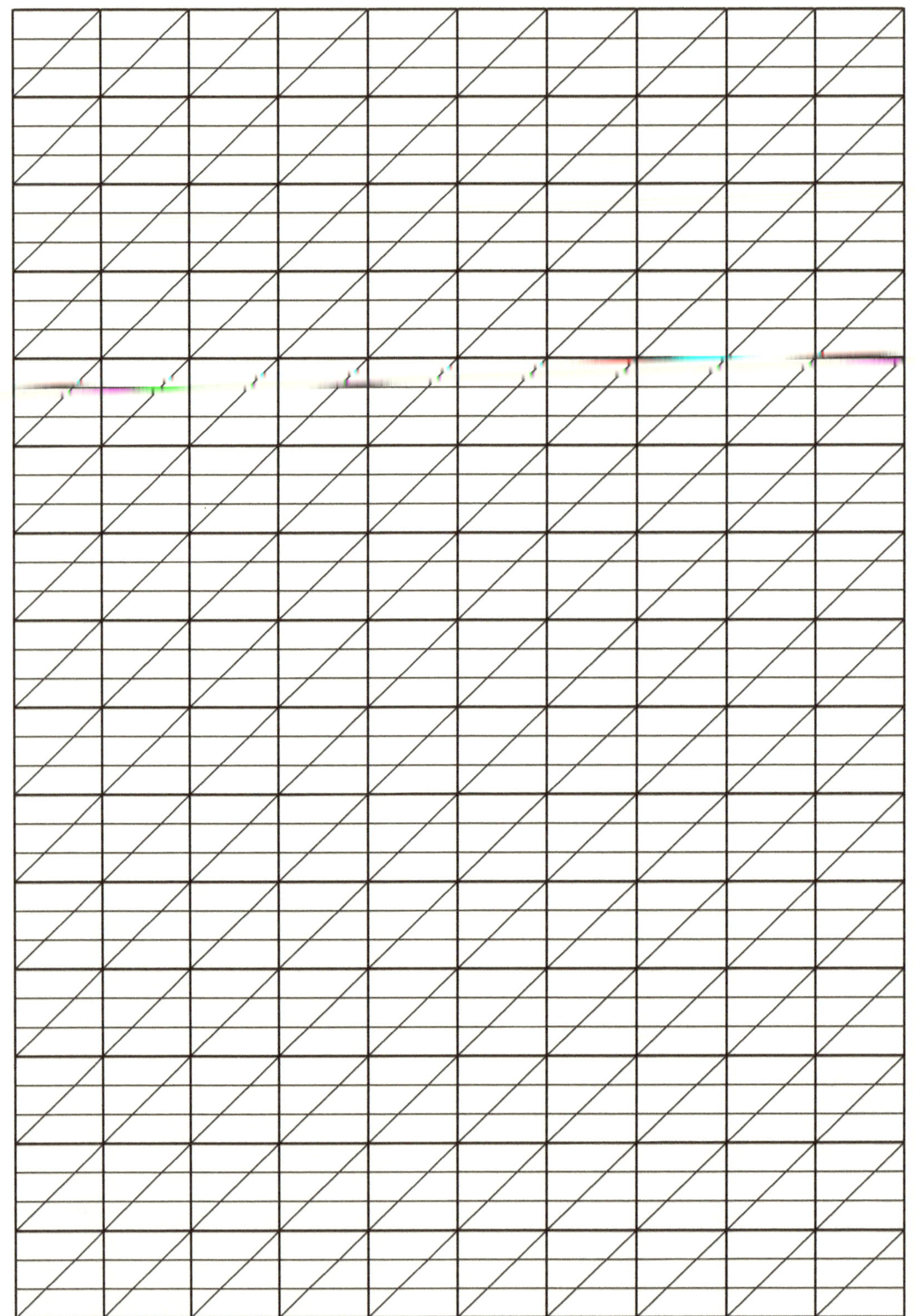

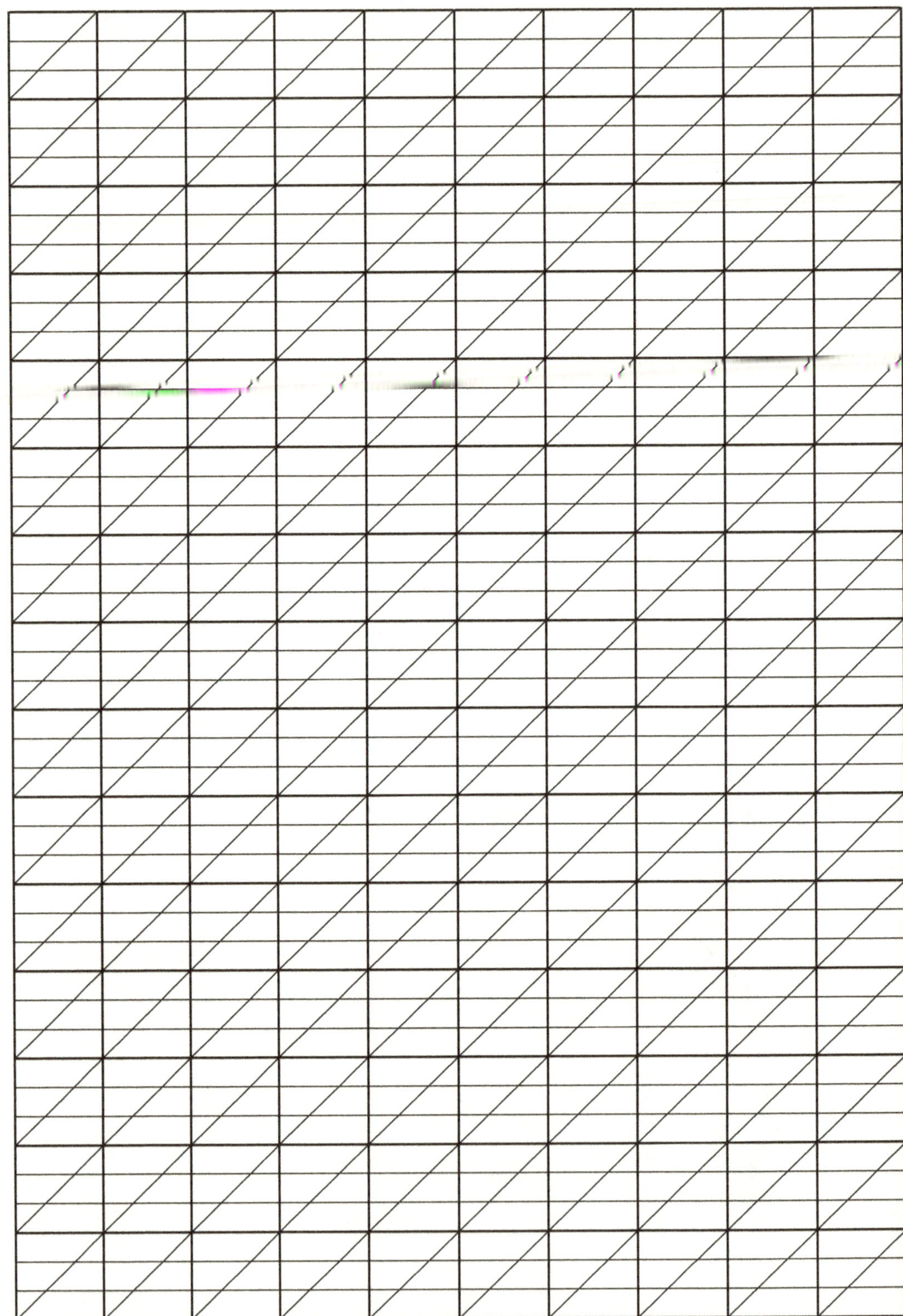

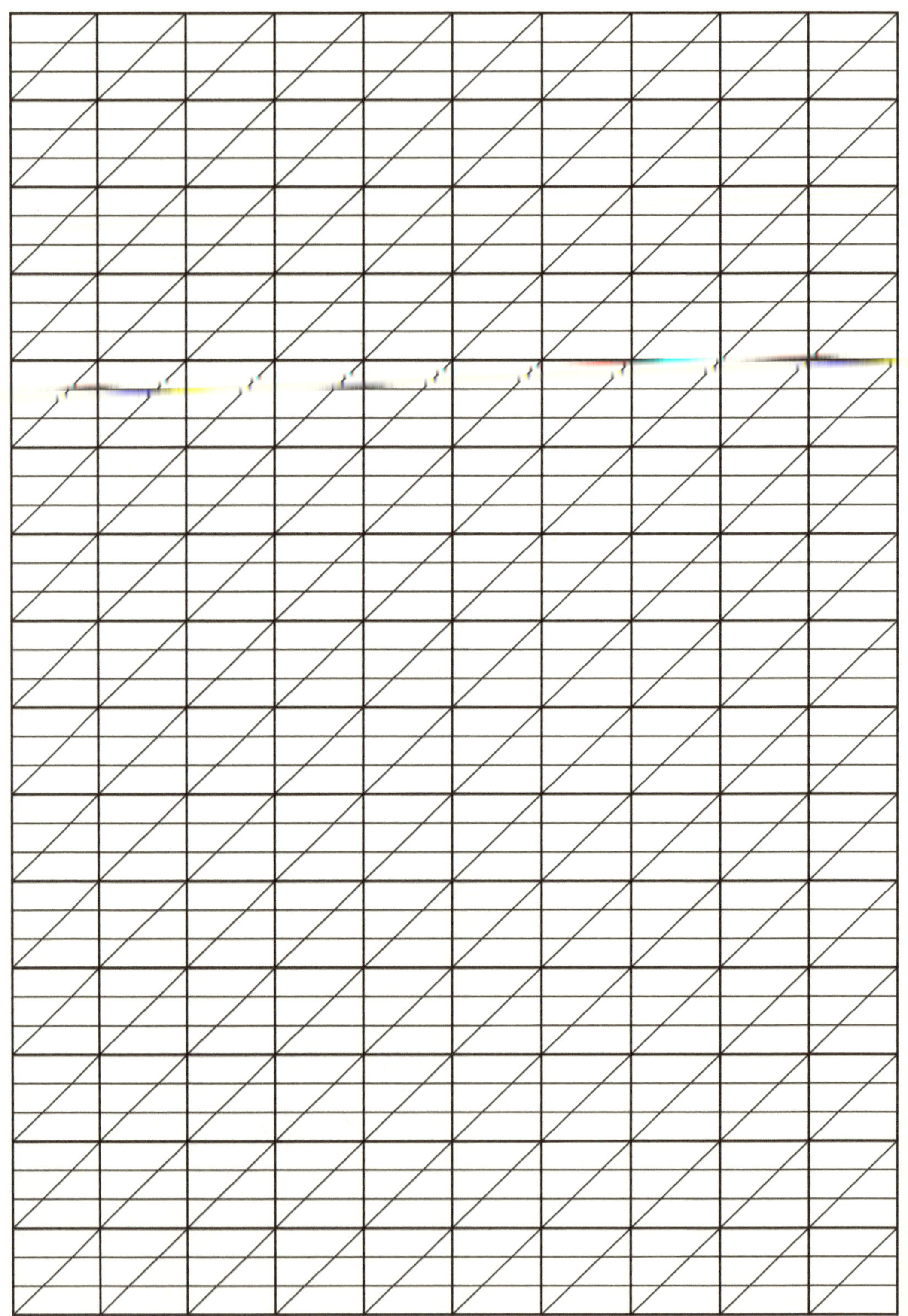

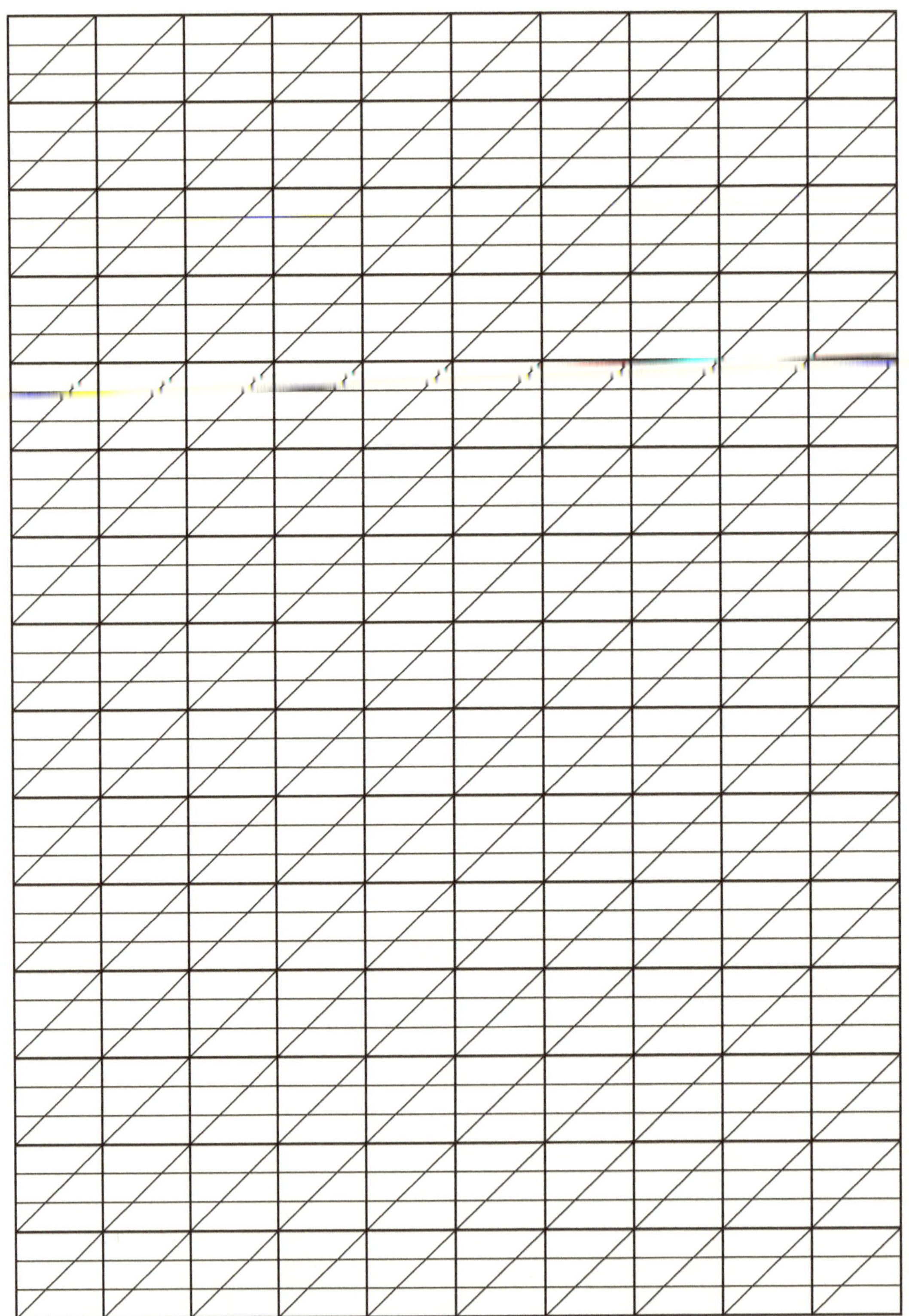

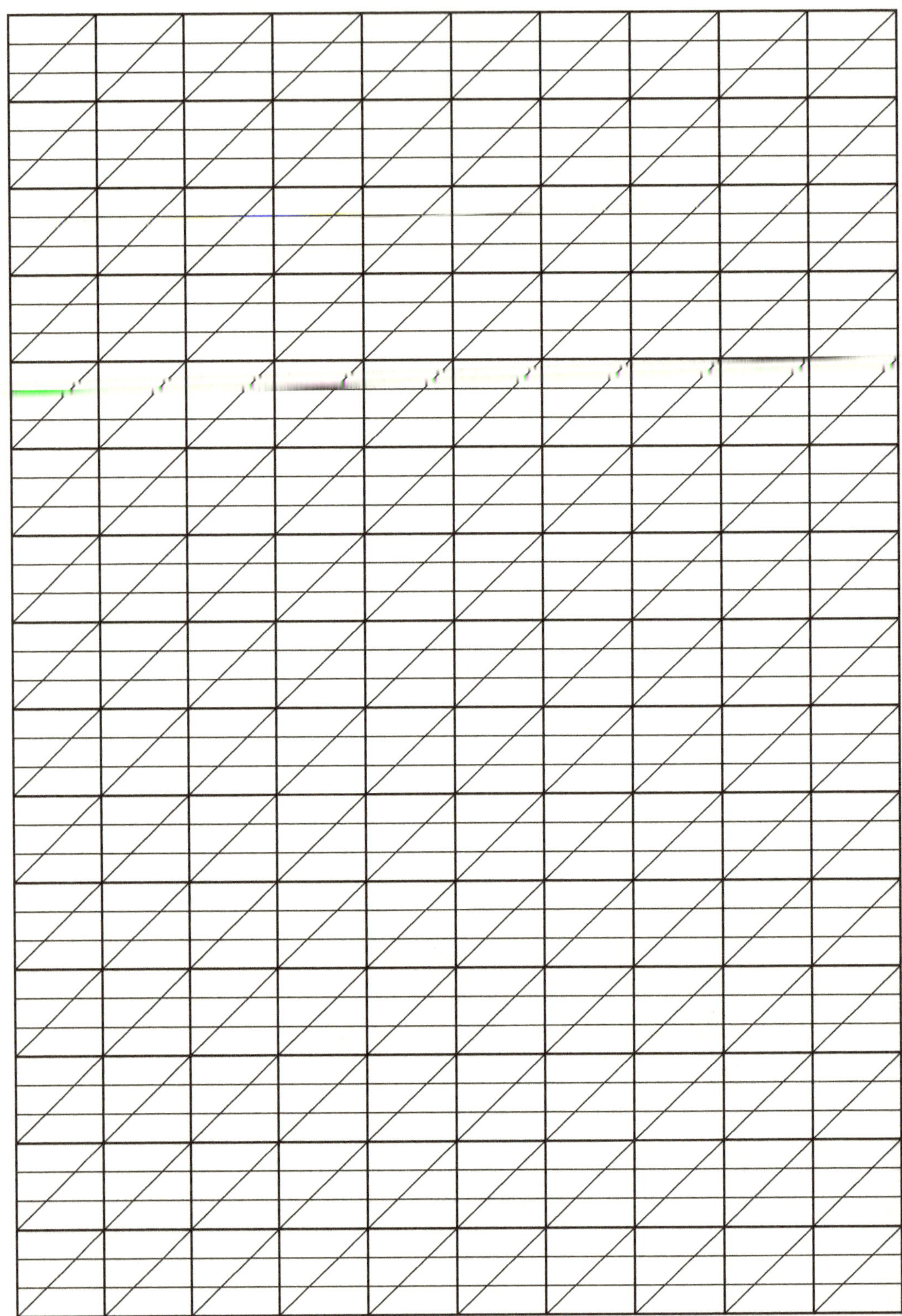